Snippets and Short Tails

Tricia Williams

Copyright (c) 2015 Tricia Williams
All rights reserved

For everyone who encouraged me and
supported me, thank you

My life has been very varied; I've lived in too many places; I've done too many jobs.

On the other hand I've met lots of fascinating people.

I've been a mother, an IT geek, a chef, a cleaner, a teacher, a senior manager, a singer, a statistician, a party planner and so much more.

And through it all I told stories. Most were lost in the mists of time, ephemeral tales told as bedtime stories or made-up to while away long journeys.

But with access to a laptop some of my more recent stories survived.

So from my life of chaos here are a few snippets - some fiction, some fact, some interesting and, maybe, some funny.

Contents

Fiction and Fantasy..6
    Brief tails...6
  Landing..7
  And Repeat..10
  Young Lilly..14
  Training Dragons is Easy..................................20
  My Childhood Home..22
  I Did It All..27
  Knitting for Love...29
  The Man of Her Dreams...................................32
  Here You Are My Dear.....................................37
  Science Moves On...41
  Winter in July..46
  Listing Now...47
  Always Running..49
  What Do Mermaids Eat?...................................51
  My Best Enemy...53
  Flicker..56
  Safety First...59
  Revenge is a Dish...60
  Fourteen Minus One...62
Give Me Three Words and I Will Tell a Story..........63
  That Thing 64
  Cat, Butterfly, Dragon 65
  A Nice Dress...67
  A Nice Dress Too..70
  Conversations...72
  If Only...75
NaNoWriMo Challenge: 76
Almost Non-Fiction...77
  The What Do You Call It?................................78

- Venturing Out..79
- Why Has the Toaster Played Such an Important Role in Weddings?..81
- An Endless Circle..84
- They knew they had the answer......................86
- Life, Facts and Thoughts....................................89
  - Myths and Science - The Impact of the Observer.90
  - Not Learning to Drive......................................92
  - A TWO HUNDRED PER CENT INCREASE!!............94
  - Flying Home the Long Way...........................96
  - Warning, Invisible Monsters in the Dysk!!!........98
  - Moar Invisible Monsters................................102
  - Dancing in the Forests of My Mind................104
  - Real Milk..106
  - Winter in July...107
  - I struggled to learn to read 108
  - Bread and Butter..109
  - Exploring South Yorkshire............................112
  - What, No 'Ats?...113
  - Ouch!...115
  - Work, 1970s Style..116
  - The Mighty Heap..118
  - Acquiring Your First Cat...............................120
  - Shared Gremlins?...121
- And Finally a Few Filks.....................................122
  - Wights...122
  - Big Hunter...123
  - Dreams..124

Fiction and Fantasy

Brief tails

One of my cats has a long thin tail. When it lashes from side to side against my leg it feels like a whip.

My other cat has a thick bushy tail. He likes to wave it proudly, puffed up and voluminous - Until I bathe him, and his thick tail disappears to be replaced by a skinny, truncated, bony appendage.

Landing

I could see the runabout was coming down too fast; at that rate it would hit the edge of the field and probably explode.

I shouted into the com, "Reduce speed, man! You'll never make it in one piece. Reduce your speed!"

There was no reply, but after a few secs the small craft was slowing a bit. I sat back in my chair and tried to relax my tense muscles. Why did all the newbies choose my landing field to practise on? Why was it always during my shift?

As the runabout touched down I handed over to the sub, then headed for the gate. I was determined to give this one a piece of my mind.

The suited figure was already in the airlock, but hadn't even pressed the daggone button. I banged on the inner door and pointed. Had to do it twice before he reacted and then he pressed it cautiously as if it would bite. The airlock released him into the decon tunnel, but again the idiot just stood there.

"Get on with it!, I yelled. "Walk towards me." and again he waited until I added some (reasonably polite) gestures to the message, before slowly putting one foot out, then the other. He was acting as if he'd never learnt to walk.

Bad enough getting all the novice pilots, but space-sick ones were the worst hell.

He finally made it through the first level of decon, although he'd stopped when the jets started, and I'd nearly yelled myself hoarse to get him going again.

By now I'd got my own suit on and headed to the second decon section, determined to help speed him up with some more direct physical help. In fact if he didn't speed up I was going to drag him out!

I got into second decon first, and then started the pantomime again to get him to join me.

As soon as he was in and the door locked, I pulled him under the jets. A second sluicing of the outer suit was fast enough even for me, but trying to get him out of his suit for the full decon made him panic. Every time I got near him he pulled away; you'd think he'd never seen a girl in a spacesuit before.

Well I wasn't going to risk any bugs by taking my helmet off first, so I reached up and clicked the tags on his headsuit.

"Up! Get it off!" I yelled, accompanied by violent lifting movements. And he finally nodded then raised his own arms.

The head visor was still dark, so there was no warning before the headsuit lifted up quickly to reveal a sickly, pale face with mud coloured fuzz on top.

I jumped back. My Hoy, he's brought in a plague!

And I was stuck in here with him until the medics could sort him out. I closed my eyes to shut out the dreadful sight. But I couldn't stop the high-pitched sounds he was making.

"Greetings, I am from Earth."

By Hoy, he sounds in agony! Whatever he had I desperately hoped he hadn't infected me.

And Repeat

I woke slowly, first feeling the discomfort, then the pressure of my bladder, then the pain overtook all.

A gentle voice said, "Here is your morning tea my dear," as a mug is placed near my hand. Then almost unnoticed, a prick in my arm. "Your pain relief will help soon, just try to lie still for a few minutes."

But I could not, as other body functions cried louder. I struggled to sit up and rolled carefully on my side. Firm hands offered support as I slowly stood. Then, still supported, I moved one foot forward, then the other. Each step was a little easier until I was slowly shuffling towards the freshroom.

I decided to leave washing myself and dressing until later, and was helped back to my bed. Lying down again brought a little more relief, and at last I was ready for my morning drink.

The first mouthful was bitter, but hot, the second a delicious easing in my throat. I gulped the rest down, and lay back to recover from my morning exertions.

I woke slowly, first feeling the discomfort, then waiting for the pressure and pain. But there was not so much pain. I opened my eyes and saw the mug by my bed. This must be my second awakening today.

I gently stretched tight muscles, trying to move each joint without triggering the stabbing pains that would make today a 'bad day'.

Even this quiet noise was noticed. Another mug appeared on the table. "Here is more tea," said a voice behind me.

I waited a moment but there was no more sound. Again I sipped, then gulped down the welcome liquid. Next, sitting up a bit more easily, I clicked the handcon. The screen lit to a scene of a summer beach; swimmers jumping into water, dolphins playing with a ball. Just a happy tale to give comfort. If I wanted news of the people in the dome I'd have to find a 'real' channel. (The providers moved them every day, hiding from those who thought real news was bad for our health.)

I was too tired to search just yet. Which was lucky as the silent hand reached out with a plate. Followed by "Breakfast dear, don't let it get cold'."

And there was my toast, glistening with butter, carefully cut into small rectangles. Another mug followed, this time with the delicious smell of coffee.

Breakfast was perfect, just the right amount of butter on hot toast, smooth strong coffee covered by white foam. Was I disloyal to yearn for something else? A fake bacon roll? Or nutty muesli? But the toast was good even if perfection was boring after a while.

I woke slowly, first feeling the discomfort, then waiting for the pressure and pain. But there was not so much pain. I opened my eyes and saw the mug by my bed. This must be my second awakening today.

No, I wasn't hungry and there was an errant crumb of toast in my hand. So I'd had breakfast. This was my third waking.

I sipped the warm tea, not so thirsty but enjoying the taste and smell.

As soon as I finished the mug was removed and the hand returned with a damp wipe. My hands were carefully cleansed, removing the crumb of toast. I needed another sign.

I woke slowly, first feeling the discomfort, then waiting for the pressure and pain. But there was not so much pain. I opened my eyes and saw the mug by my bed. This must be my second awakening today.

I concentrated hard; was this still morning? No way to tell from the light as the window was a fake, just another vidscreen. I thought I remembered toast, but there were no crumbs and my mouth tasted of spearmint.

Ah that was the sign I needed! If my teeth had been cleaned then this was the fourth awakening.

I didn't bother to drink the tea this time. I needed to try to stay awake and I always slipped back into sleep after their drinks.

A voice behind me. "You did not drink your tea. Do you want a fresh mug now?"

"No," I mumble. The mug disappears.

I start my stretching exercises again. I am determined that today I will get up and walk alone into the bathroom. I will have a cool refreshing shower instead of the wipes. I will get dressed. I may even ask to be taken to a real window so I can see the grass and a real sky.

Halfway through the movements there is the wipe, gently cleansing me. I try to protest but it continues to move.

I woke slowly, first feeling the discomfort, then waiting for the pressure and pain. But there was not so much pain. I opened my eyes and saw the mug by my bed. This must be my second awakening today.

But no. I search my memory and then around me and realise it cannot be. There is mild hunger, little thirst and under my arm is a piece of cloth.

This is my fifth awakening. I am determined this time it will last longer than a few minutes. I ignore the mug even though I really want to taste the hot warmth. I carefully and quietly stretch my arms and legs. Not too much so as not to disturb It.

But in vain. The arm appears with a cup, covered by a baby's lid. "Here is your soup my dear." I try to refuse it, but the insistent hand pushes the spout to my mouth and a little soup trickles in. Suddenly my hunger grows and I drink.

I sense the hand moving back, and reappearing with another wipe.

I woke slowly, first feeling the discomfort, then the pressure of my bladder, then the pain overtook all.

A gentle voice said, "Here is your morning tea my dear," as a mug is placed near my hand. Then almost unnoticed a prick in my arm. "Your pain relief will help soon, just try to lie still for a few minutes."

Young Lilly

"Yes," I say, trying to smile through gritted teeth, "it's a beautiful picture".

I sit back and watch my father proudly show off his favourite photos from the mantelpiece. Carefully picking each one up and recounting the story behind the pose. There are no photos of me up there, mine are hidden behind plant pots or carefully 'forgotten', left in drawers.

I hate her. I hate everything she stands for; I hate my parents obsession with her. Everywhere in the room she poses in the pictures, slim, young, unlined. So confident, with all the world at her feet. She didn't make the mistakes I made, she didn't fail and fall. She wasn't fat and greying. She was the ideal daughter.

I sit with the false smile on my face, thinking about the picture my father holds. I remember that day so well. She was wearing a new dress, a slim size 10; tall and glowing with happiness. Another perfect day in her life.

It started with the cards, a large pile by her chair at breakfast; symbols of the love and admiration of family and friends. She laughed as she opened the one from her latest boyfriend. "Oh look what Danny sent!" And it was passed around for Father and Mother to read the cloying message inside.

Then on to try on the new dress, white silk and lace swirling around her as she posed for another set of pictures. I barely remember my father without that camera, waiting for yet another opportunity to catch his brilliant Lilly again; and again.

Now he has picked up the one with her holding her certificate. Proudly looking at the camera with her impressive list of exams held high. He boasts that she was top of her year; that she sailed thorough exams with ease while serving as head girl, playing netball and winning the trophies that sit in the specially made cupboard beside me.

This is a well-rehearsed diversion from the endless pictures. A small break as he gathers himself to open the cupboard and lift out her cups and plaques. Passing each one around the room as he tells of each glorious event and how she excelled at sport, won speaking contests, was the best prefect 'ever' and sang solos with the school choir.

It seems too much for one frail girl to hold. But I can't forgive her. I can never forgive her. I want to cry out: "but I am here. What about me!". But I sit silent, grasping a cold cup of tea hard, in case I throw it at the cupboard and scream out my hate.

Sometimes I think of stealing down in the night and emptying all the trophies into a bin bag, sneaking them out and throwing them away. Leaving a door open on the way back. Then waiting quietly in my bedroom until my father discovers the loss. I'd need to practise look of surprise, and the look of sorrow – while holding in my glee.

At last he comes to the ends of the trophies, and there is an uncomfortable silence as his guests look at me. Waiting for something, anything to explain me; the ghost at the feast. But he doesn't even notice; too wrapped in his memories. One of the women shuffles uncomfortably and nudges her husband. "Umm, sorry we didn't realise it was so late, we need to go I'm afraid." At which they all stand and walk to the door, eager to leave the silence; avoiding me as they mutter their goodbyes.

After all, what is there to say to me? I am the failure; the misfit in the room. The reminder that not all things turn out so perfectly. I leave the room, her shrine, and walk quietly to my bedroom. The only part tin this house where I have any place. Here are my memories, my photos. I sit on the bed, hugging a pillow to my face and cry.

I cry for the loss of my confidence, for my father's refusal to love me, to let me be the person I am.

It wasn't always like this. I remember the excitement of setting off on the great adventure, my first days at university. Immersed in literature and believing I would be the next famous author, waiting to be discovered. I introduced myself to the others in my lodgings, and we went to our new 'local'. We talked about our subject choices, and started to separate into interest groups. I was the only one studying Creative writing and English literature, but I tried to keep up with everyone's discussions. And I told them about my novel, a story of a young girl's journey through life.

I arrived at my first tutor group, my shiny folder boldly embossed with my name, to find there was only one seat left, at the back. I walked through the group, my head high. I expected to enjoy my tutor groups, to grasp the chance to discuss my ideas and my views of others. But somehow it didn't quite work out. The tutor started a discussion on the merits of the Existentialist genre compared with the Novel of ideas. And I was lost by the first sentence.

That initial meeting coloured the whole of my first term. I sat in groups who earnestly debated subjects and concepts I had no knowledge of; but I was too shocked and embarrassed to ask. I retreated into the corner and pretended to write notes; though all I scribbled was nonsense. I avoided the group outside, hiding in my room claiming I was writing my great novel and needed to be alone.

At Christmas I went home. I sat on the train wondering how I could tell my parents how I had failed, but knowing I wouldn't. At the front door I braced myself, stuck a smile on my face and opened the door shouting: "I'm home everyone!".

And that was when it started, the Great Pretence. Of course I was successful, of course I outshone everyone else on my course. My tutors adored me; I was getting A's on every essay. My father could be proud of me.

Going back to the second term was so hard. I dreaded the walk from the door to my room, with my flatmates asking about my holiday and taking about the exams due to start next week. I hadn't submitted a single piece of work yet, and knew I was going to fail my exams.

I shut myself in my room and desperately opened the dusty books. But I couldn't even get through a page of the text. I didn't know anything, I couldn't understand anything.

On the day of the first exam, I caught a bus out of town. I had no idea where I went, but it was away from the university and my parents' expectations. I stayed away four days, until I ran out of money. Then I returned to a letter from my tutor, asking where I was, was I ill, did I have a sick note? There was no answer to give him, so I hid in my room again, waiting for the blow to fall.

Two days after, he appeared at my door; if I couldn't explain my absence they had no choice but to ask me to leave. I packed, and endured another train ride home. I put on a mask of confidence and at the door, I called out, "Only me. Sorry but there is a nasty bug going around and they told us to go home." And so the lies started. Not just a pretence, but lies. The university was infected with flu, that turned into meningitis, then the long delay while it was disinfected.

When I finally ran out of stories about the epidemics, I started travelling. I'd go out on Monday, return on Thursday, telling my parents that my flatmates were too noisy and it was easier to work at home between classes. I camped on friends' floors, saying that I only had classes on Thursdays and Fridays this term, but if I went home my parents would expect me to help them instead of studying.

I managed to last until the end of the summer term. Then I got my 'holiday job', working in a supermarket and officially living back home. At the end of summer, I said the course was starting late, then later. Then I said I was swapping to a more intense course as this one was too light.

It all ended when my father realised no one had asked for this year's fees. He called the University, who told him I'd left ten months before.

That night we had the Talk. My parents sat across from me asking 'why'? I don't know which was worse for them, my academic failure or my life revealed as a common shop assistant. Then they retreated to the past. Their friends and neighbours heard constantly about the school successes, but the present me was never mentioned. I just sat like a pale ghost, endlessly hearing about the Lilly who lived my childhood.

For me, all my past prizes and trophies meant nothing. I am still here! I am me, now! But my parents never forgave me for failing their dreams.

I hate young Lilly. I wish she'd never been born.

Training Dragons is Easy

Yesterday I'd finished my painting of the unicorn and waved it goodbye. Today I was starting a new picture.

I placed a prepared canvas on my easel and picked up a clean palette. Then I closed my eyes and tried to imagine the finished colours.

My dragon would have deep greens and blues for its scales, and turquoise eyes. I would need greys and blacks for the shadows, plus some white to lighten the side facing the sun. If it were flaming then I'd need reds and oranges, but I decided it would be sleeping with its mouth closed, so no need to prepare those.

But, no. My dragon has such lovely eyes, they must be seen. I will paint the eyes half-shut; a sleepy dragon.

I loaded my palette with whites, black, blues and yellows – enough to make all the colours I'd imagined. Then I opened the north-facing doors so I could see the forest outside. This would be my background.

I selected a quiet piece of meditation music for the player, before picking up my charcoal to do the first rough sketch.

Sometimes approaching the blank canvas is too difficult; my hand freezes and the first stroke fails. Today I am confident as the broad marks place my dragon across the frame of the canvas.

The head is turned towards me on the left, the body curved around, the tail fading into the distance on the right. As I sketch, a grey mist swirls from the trees into the foreground; it mimics my drawing within the frame of the wide doorway.

I step back and consider the sketch. Yes, the dragon's body is placed just where I saw it in my mind.

I return to the easel and begin to add colour, a mix of clear greens and blues on the sunny side, darkening into deeper colours towards the back and tail. Each scale has a hint of silver where the sunlight hits it. I paint the claws dark, almost black. Then I concentrate on the head. The half-closed turquoise eyes, staring directly at me, outlined in white, then deep blue eyelids.

As I paint the mist outside thickens and colours emerge. It is if the mist draws from the trees' green leaves and dark trunks; then from the deep blue of a darkening sky. As I paint the last strokes of the eyes, the mist coalesces and my dragon is born.

I put down my palette and brush and step out to meet her. She is pleasantly sleepy, resting in the sun and listening to our music. She welcomes my strokes, replicating the movements of my hand painting across her head and back.

I lie down next to her and rest my head on her arm; I am pleasantly sleepy myself now after a busy day creating my tame dragon.

My Childhood Home

I always thought my childhood was normal. Well, young children do, don't they? I lived with my mother, her two sisters and their elderly aunt in a three storey house on the edge of town. The house was full of interesting corners and odd stairs, brilliant for hide and seek. My room had a large cupboard full of my mother's old toys and there were trees to climb in the garden.

In the morning I had lessons with Mother. Once I'd learnt to read my Aunts helped, providing classes in mathematics and science. I didn't even realise that other children attended schools.

I spent a lot of time on my own; there were no other children in the houses near me and the adults in my home were usually too busy to play with me. So I did what many only children do, I had other friends.

There was Polly, who liked to play with my mother's dolls. She could spend hours dressing them up and holding pretend tea parties. When she'd finished she would fold up the clothes, wash the 'dishes' and tidy everything away. I really liked having Polly round when my room got too messy. I never got into trouble when I was with Polly.

When I was bored with the dolls there was Suey. She loved climbing trees in the back garden and always wore jeans. She'd help me climb through the thick hedge at the back so we could pet the horses in the field. Once she even crawled through the fence and rode one of the ponies up and down. I was too nervous to join her, but it looked like a lot of fun.

However, I didn't see Suey for a while after the stolen ride. Mother told me that Suey had been bad and was not allowed out for four weeks.

But I still had my third friend, George. He was older than me; taller and stronger and faster. But he never minded waiting for me when we ran home. With George I learned to make bows and arrows and we stalked the grey tom cat through the trees when he was hunting.

And then there was Al, who taught me to speak a special language that we could share, took me to meet his family, and laughed with me as I struggled to learn how to eat their food with just my fingers. No plunging my hands into the shared bowl but a piece of bread and a careful dip which, when done correctly, resulted in a mouthful of delicious food. My first attempts only gave me a hint of the juices, or worse a soggy mess sliding onto the table!

My last long summer at home seemed endless. Every day if it was sunny I would be outside with Suey or George. On the wet cold days Polly would happily play for hours with the old toys from the cupboard. And once a week if I was lucky there would be Al ready to take me into a world of foreign scents and smiling faces.

I loved my home, and my family, and I'd have stayed there forever. But at the end of the summer Mother took me aside one evening.

"My darling, you are growing up fast and growing out of our lessons. It is time for you to go to a place where there are better teachers. There are places called schools, where the best teachers gather groups of children and teach them all together.

"Your Aunts and I have decided that you must attend one of these schools from September. It will be a big change for you, but I know you will make me proud."

She hugged me and smiled, but the smile wasn't as big as her usual smiles.

I was too stunned at first to understand everything she said that first night, but after she had repeated it all she tucked me into bed with a promise to talk more in the morning.

I thought I would never get to sleep; my mind was racing trying to make sense of this sudden decision to send me away. Had I been too noisy playing with George, did Polly forget to tidy away all the toys, had Suey been bad again? Or even worse was it my fault, had I caused this?

I must have gone to sleep at last, as I woke to another warm sunny day. I jumped out of bed, planning the route George and I could map out this afternoon. Then I remembered Mother's words.

Instead of dancing down the stairs, my feet reluctantly took each step. But however slowly they dragged eventually I reached the bottom and had to pin on a smile to greet my family.

"Hello Darling," Mother said, with another tight smile, "Did you sleep well?"

"Yes," I managed, avoiding meeting her eyes.

Everyone tried to behave as if this was just another ordinary morning. But the meal seemed to last for hours.

At last breakfast was over and Mother and the Aunts walked with me to the teaching room. We all sat and there was a pause.

Then Mother began. "You must have lots of questions? You can ask anything you want, but first I will remind you of our chat last night."

She repeated her story about me growing up, about other children and the schools they attended instead of lessons with Aunts and Mothers. It made no more sense to me the third time.

I asked the questions that had haunted me in the night.

"Don't you love me any more? Did I do something bad? Why me? Why now?"

They all assured me that of course they loved me, no, this was not a punishment, it was time for me to meet other children and broaden my life. That they were doing this for me.

And finally the questions and answers stopped.

A week later I said goodbye to Polly, Suey and George; I'd left a message for Al. Then I hugged the Aunts, trying to be a 'big girl' and not cry or run up to my room and hide. Mother and I sat in the back of the taxi, and once more she attempted to persuade me that I was on the way to an exciting new opportunity. I just nodded and closed my eyes.

When the taxi stopped there was a large gate blocking the road. Beyond it was a grey building, surrounded by neat lawns and trees.

The gate opened, and the taxi drove up to the house. I saw there were three children waiting to greet me on the bottom of a large flight of steps.

"Hello," one of them said. "You must be Rose. My name is Suey and these are Polly and George. Welcome to our school."

I Did It All

I was in the lab, testing for gunpowder residue from his hands. Then I heard the timer, and walked over to the DNA machine; the sample I'd prepared confirmed my theory. Yes, I had noted at the crime scene, while declaring the butler was dead, that his wife looked flustered.

She had touched him at some point in the last five hours. I grabbed my gun and car keys, drove back to the house and interviewed her. I started off softly, establishing a rapport and sympathising with her loss. Then I came down heavily, forced her into a corner and shouted, "I know you did it, I'm taking you down."

She burst into tears, but I wasn't moved; all my suspects cried.

I got out the handcuffs and dragged her to the car. It took a while to force her through the rear door, but finally she was in and I was driving back to the station.

"Lock her up!" I ordered as I rushed past; I was nearly out of time to stir the gel before it set. Luckily, the gel was fine, and in no time I was shooting the gun from the crime scene into the quivering blocks of clear jelly. I'd managed to check the rifling before breakfast, and so now I had all the evidence together. I carefully wrapped up the residue tests, DNA analysis, the handwriting sample I'd compared with his supposed suicide note, the ballistics reports, my autopsy notes and the fingerprint reports.

Wait! I'd nearly forgotten my insect analysis! Not that it added to the evidence against her, but I liked to be thorough.

I strode back to the cells where she was waiting docilely for me to lock her up. Intentionally confusing her, I marched her instead into the interview room, set up the recorder and started phase two of the questioning.

Once she had seen my evidence, it only took ten minutes for her to break. I charged her, locked her up, wrote up my notes, stored the evidence and was ready to go home.

Enough time to finish off the pot roast and shower before my darling hubbie gets home, I thought. Then back to work at the law office, preparing my argument for her trial.

(Inspired by several USA TV crime series)

Knitting for Love

I wanted to make something special for my new love. I didn't have much money, and he already had a roomful of the latest gadgets. And some lovely designer label clothes, way beyond my budget.

He did have a tatty, old scarf, that his mother knitted for him years ago. He wore it everywhere.

I decided to knit him a new scarf. I bought some wool and a pair of needles, and a friend showed me how to get started.

Knit one
purl one
knit one
purl one

I hadn't even got to the end of the second row and my hands were beginning to stiffen up. Maybe I was holding the needles too hard? I tried to relax, and one needle escaped, and then so did several loops of wool.

Bother, I'd almost managed to get the hang of putting the stitches onto the needle, but I had no idea how to sort out a mess of loops lying across my lap. Every time I tried to catch a loop, two more slipped off instead.

At this point I was struggling to recall why I even wanted to learn to knit.

Eventually I took all the stitches off, rolled up the wool and started again.

There, I have forty neat stitches waiting to grow into neat rows. I start again on row two. In goes the needle.

Well actually it doesn't. The first stitches are now so tight there is no room for a knitting needle. I try pushing harder, but no way is that needle going into this tight, neat stitch.

Off come the loops from the needle again. I rewound the ball of wool, not so neat by now.

Cast on
one, two,
three, four
five, six.

I tried not to wind the wool so tight; difficult, as it seemed to have a life of its own and the loops weren't staying in place on my slippery new needles.

Twenty, twenty one, there goes a stitch off the needle. I swear it moved by itself this time. I still couldn't get the hang of picking up, so I took all the wool off yet again. I rolled it up onto the ball, which looked a little lumpy.

Cast on
one, two,
three, four
five, six ...

I started on row two. This time the stitches were loose, but not actually falling off as long as I kept the pointy end of the needle up a bit.

Knit one
purl one

knit one
purl one

There, I'd almost finished row two! But I could hear the phone ringing. Should I risk putting down the knitting needles?

The phone rings on. I carefully put down my knitting and answer it. A double glazing salesman.

Back to my chair. I look at the heap of wool and plastic and carefully start to pick it up. I'm left with one naked needle and a pile of loops. I think they are grinning at me.

I definitely can't remember why I wanted to do this.

And I won't do it.

The Man of Her Dreams

She lay on her bed imagining the room of her dreams; it was her birthday in less than a week and she was desperately hoping that she'd done enough.

She'd first seen it on a trip into town a few months ago, and couldn't take her eyes off the shop window. It was the best bedroom ever; the Princess Pretty suite in all its glory. She'd dragged her parents over to admire it, and told them it was all she'd ever want. If they bought it for her, she would never ask for another thing. But they just smiled and said her bedroom was fine as it was.

She tried nagging her mother, she tried smiling at her father while wearing her prettiest dress, the one he said made her look like a princess. But they still said it was too expensive.

She spent a whole weekend doing the washing up without being asked. She met her father at the door every evening for four whole days, hung up his coat and made him a drink; she was his perfect princess. But they still refused to give in.

Finally, last week her father had relented a little and said they might, just might, be able to buy the Princess Pretty bed. The bed was a four poster, with pink painted wood and pink and white lacy curtains. It was beautiful.

So now she would have a pretty lacy pink bed, with a boring brown cupboard and blue curtains. Hopefully as soon as her mother realised how awful it looked, she would get Dad to buy the rest of the suite, and new curtains and bedding to match. Then she would have the bedroom of her dreams and everything would be perfect.

She would wear her best pink dress and entertain all her friends with tales of life as a princess.

She closed her eyes and dreamed in pink.

A week later she was showing off her pink room to envious friends. They dressed up in their princess outfits and danced around. She was so happy.

Four years later she hated the frilly pink bedroom. It was too embarrassing to bring her friends home in case they saw it. She pretended her room had a bed-settee for lounging on in the day, and dark cream walls 'because the parents wouldn't agree to yellow last year'.

She'd asked them to redecorate, but they had reminded her how much she'd wanted the Princess Pretty suite and how much it had cost. She started to plan a campaign to change her daddy's mind.

But she was distracted by meeting the boy of her dreams.

He filled all the attributes on her list: he was two years older, had a part-time job and a motorbike. He was tall, dark-haired and slim. He was gorgeous. And all her friends envied her when he asked her out.

After their second date, he called her his 'little princess' and she felt cherished and happy. She liked to go to places where she could wear a dress or skirt; the feeling of the skirt swirling around her helped her imagine they were a prince and his princess, visiting their adoring people. She also felt protected and loved when she was with him, tucked under his arm.

He wanted her to learn to ride his bike, but she hated the noise and smell. He talked about science and university, she wanted poetry. But still he was her perfect prince and she was his princess. She lay in bed, with her eyes shut, and dreamed about them getting married and living happily ever after. She wore a long white dress with ruffles, a glittering tiara and carried orange blossom.

Then one day he said they needed to talk. He said he was sorry, but they didn't share the same interests and he thought she would be happier with someone who didn't like building bikes or tramping through the woods at weekends.

She spent the next two years reading about the wives of the famous, and learning from her 'mags' how to be the perfect business wife. This time her prince would have a future, and money. Her earlier image of her prince was childish, but she knew now what would make her happy. And once she was married she could finally get rid of the remnants of the Princess Pretty suite.

She practised her new skills on her father, who still called her his little princess and bought her trinkets. He agreed she didn't need a career, and paid for a cheap version of a finishing school.

At last she was ready; she had done a cordon bleu course and learned how to fold napkins into six different shapes. She had prepared a suitable wardrobe of pretty summer dresses, and curled her long hair. She booked tickets for the ballet and opera.

It only took her two weeks to find the man of her dreams. He was tall, with dark hair, and only ten years older than her. He was intelligent and cultured. He did not have a motor bike.

He worked long hours, but he liked to eat supper with her and let his chauffeur take her home when he was working late. And of course he called her his 'princess'.

He bought her an enormous sapphire ring, to match her eyes. She acted as his hostess at important dinners parties, where he wooed the business community. With the men she smiled and waited on them carefully. But when he entertained the women business colleagues, she had no role. She couldn't take part in the conversations, and she felt silly waiting on them.

Eventually she realised that she was bored with her prince. He worked at least ten hours every day, and had no time to take her out or sit and read poetry to her. The pleasant suppers had stopped; he was always too busy.

She hadn't invested all that time to be ignored. She needed a prince, not a workaholic robot.

She started reading the magazines again, studying the advice for singles. And she realised that she needed to understand something about business and work in order to interest the right man.

She took an introductory philosophy course and, to her surprise, she enjoyed it. She learnt to drive, so she could get to college without waiting for buses. Daddy brought her a small car.

She enrolled next on a technology course, and discovered she had an aptitude for spotting problems and analysing data. And all that planning over the years made her very organised.

She still went out to parties and clubs every weekend, but sometimes bought her own drinks.

During the holidays she started planning her next move, first listing what she wanted in a husband, and then a list of things she didn't want. To her astonishment, the second list was longer. It was much longer.

And the Man of her Dreams disappeared into a mist.

Here You Are My Dear

The new laboratory was white and shiny. All the large machines were carefully spaced with plenty of worktops and expanses of floor around each; everything else was neatly packed away in labelled cupboards.

My manager was still standing in the doorway, proudly indicating the room. I realised he'd stopped talking, and clearly expected me to speak.

"It's very clean," I managed, trying to smile.

"Yes! We put in updated versions of all the old stuff you had, plus a few upgrades. You'll be able to work much more efficiently now." He smiled at me.

"Thank you," I muttered, "I'll get started now if you do not mind." And I moved away from him towards the first metallic block.

He took the hint and left. I let my fake smile relax and looked around in despair. All my familiar tools were gone, even the ones I'd had specially designed for the latest project. In their place were tools from well-known household names. Fine no doubt for tinkering with a plug, but nothing like my specialist tools, carefully collected over years.

I turned to the larger items. There was a brand new DNA analyser, shiny and smart; it attracted managers by the lower cost and the glossy sales pitch. Unfortunately it wasn't as accurate as my old Belogen.

Next to it was another glossy new machine. This one was intended to identify and match odours. However, the new machine, a Hoovanose, only analysed about 200,000 odours. My adapted Odouranalyser could identify at least 950,000.

It became all too much, I could not bear to look at any more of his 'improvements'. I walked over to the lab desk and sat. I sat on a new chair that squeaked as I moved, at a clear desk where the lab books for tests I had been working on should be.

I opened the drawers, but they only contained tissues and hand wipes (What!). Then I saw the orange note on my desk monitor. "It's all in here!" proclaimed the note. I recognised my manager's handwriting. Not that we saw it often; he was an avid proponent of the paperless-office.

I turned on the dumb terminal, logged in and found my directory.

And as I opened each file, carefully named after a lab book, my despair turned to fury. He'd had each set of notes carefully transcribed, with my sketches transformed into clip art and the 'spelling errors' corrected.

I looked at a screenful of garbage from my latest lab book; 'Na' was now 'no', the bio_sole had become Bisole (a place in Africa?) and the reference to 'LABRADOR being used in conjunction with dogs' now read 'several dogs'.

That was the final straw. I opened the cupboard labelled with a 'cute' clip art skull and found a bottle of Methyl alcohol. Perfect. There was no reason for me to ever use it and my old lab hadn't had any. If anyone knew it was on the inventory I could just plead ignorance. Not that my assumed ignorance would ever reach the depths of his stupidity.

The new system and cute labels turned out to have an advantage now; it only took me 2.5 minutes to find everything I needed. Armed with the bottle of champagne he'd supplied, no doubt expecting me to celebrate his mutilation of my work, I walked to his office.

"I am sorry, you must have thought me very rude." I spoke loudly so his clerk would hear. "I found the gift you left for me and just had to bring it over so we could celebrate together."

I placed the bottle on his desk and waited.

"Oh no, I know how excited you were and fully understood you wanted to play with your new toys!"

I tried to ungrit my teeth before replying. "Well yes, but you should celebrate with me as this was all your idea and your hard work." Another smile. Who'd have thought I could act so well?

I waited until he'd poured out the liquid into two glasses and then drained my glass.

I coughed. "That is strong. I don't usually drink any alcohol as you know, but I didn't expect it to be so strong." And I carefully slid to the floor.

I awoke several hours later in hospital.

They told me that the clerk had saved my life, after my manager had tried to persuade her to just let me sleep it off.

At the trial, the fact that he'd also not touched his own drink and her evidence of my words were the main reasons he was found guilty of attempted murder.

And the Motive? Jealousy. He'd been told to use most of this year's budget to replace the damaged items from my last little experiment; cutting back on his junkets abroad with his mistress to pay for it.

And me? I made a full recovery. I even managed to find most of my equipment in the storage warehouse. In no time my lab looked almost like old. And I hardly missed the trips abroad – he'd become too boring.

Science Moves On

Jole wasn't sure about it. He had dismissed it as another old women's tale, following on from his father's reactions to the old women. But now?

The village had a lot of old superstitions; their main use seemed to be to keep the children under control. He'd grown up with the endless sayings: "If you do that the goblins will steal you"; "If you make that face it will freeze when the Winter King sees it"; and "If you don't cool the milk immediately the Arthropods will sour it".

Then he had passed the special scholar tests and been sent away to school, and he soon learned that the old tales were nonsense; just funny stories to explain the changes that the older people couldn't understand, mixed up with scare stories to threaten children. The first made him impatient, why didn't they try to learn? The second made him angry, only monsters would do this to small babies and little toddlers.

So over the years he stayed away as much as possible. He'd return for the winter feast, and his parents' binding celebration each year, but never for other reasons. He lost touch with his early school mates, as only his later friends understood his anger and only they shared his interests now.

The gulf between the main school towns and the villages had grown wider as the scientists experimented and found new ways to describe and understand the world. They needed new machines, so industry changed around them, providing tools instead of farm implements.

The new towns still needed the food, the cloths and other goods from the villages, but at the evening discussions they talked at length about new ways to create food and how the latest materials from their labs would replace the fabrics and woods supplied by the olders.

And in the villages? Life went on, food was always needed as were their other goods. This took much of their time, especially as they had to produce food for those who no longer worked with them. Their busy lives remained simple compared to the townsfolk. Yet while their evenings were spent on discussing how to help their communities, sharing tips on developing new seeds and better stock, there was time for philosophical wondering. And time for the old stories.

The villagers knew the importance of history; if you didn't know that a great-uncle had already tried to cross breed the coo with the shept and failed then you could waste many years repeating his failure; if you remembered the family stories and went to consult the library then you could move on to a new breeding experiment.

Knowing the importance of their history, they offered copies to the folk in the new towns, who scoffed and said there was nothing in the Olders' tales for men of science.

Meanwhile the world moved on its axis and the time of the long cold was approaching. The villagers prepared as usual. They may not have any personal memories of the last cold, but their records showed it repeated every three hundred years.

The scientists in the towns noted some chilly days, but that happened every year. Yet when they remembered the villagers' tales they thought it might be good to study their sun and the other local planets again, and they added the idea to a list.

Unfortunately that list was long, and more exciting research projects attracted them.

And by now they were so remote from their roots they only noticed the serious changes in the weather when the seas began to freeze.

They set up an emergency committee, and made the climate research a priority. And Jole's daughter, now a bioscientist, was tasked with checking which of the earlier research projects might provide short-cuts. So over dinner she asked her father if any of his work might assist them.

And their discussion triggered a memory; one of the often repeated stories from his youth.

"In the old days, not long after the arrival, the settlers saw their crops grew too slowly and the waters cooled and the dinos left the area. Soon after the Winter King came to stay. The people had a little food left from the long journey and they eked it out through the endless winter. The Winter King stayed for two cycles before he left them. It took a further two cycles for the land to warm enough for their crops to grow again.

"Since then the Winter King had returned several times; and on each visit he stayed two full cycles. Food would run out, there were no new babies and the oldest would die.

"After a few visits, the historians measured the cycles and found a pattern, so now the people would plan for the Winter King's visits. The people would store food, and make warm clothes, and wait until after his visit for new babies."

Jole had dismissed this story along with the rest of his mother's tales, but maybe there was a truth somewhere within it? He decided to make a long-overdue visit home.

His mother greeted him with delight; it seemed that however much he neglected her or ridiculed her beliefs, she always forgave him. But this visit was particularly special, as for the first time since he was a young child he asked for the story about the Winter King.

"We wondered when the scientists would look up from their desks," she replied with a smile. "The story is just for the younger ones to help them understand why things must change sometimes. I think you have come to hear the adult version.

"The beginning of the story is the same. Only a few years after the settlers arrived our warm climate began to change. They endured a terrible winter that was colder than any before, and which did not lift fully for three more years.

"Then warm climate returned, and only the stories about the first settlers kept alive the history of that time. Until over three hundred years later the cold returned. And again after another three hundred years. And then again.

"Our historians added to the story, and our ancestors told it to the children. And we planned how to survive the cold season.

"Do you remember the tale of the caves? They are real. Near every village we have deep caves, so we can live nearer to the heart of the planet. We dry and store food; we let the animals die off, only storing their seed for after the freeze; and then before the cold gets too intense the whole village will move down.

"We estimate the freeze will be complete within one year from now, and our plans are made and we are ready.

"All the villages have been concerned about the scientists in the towns. Your leaders did not listen to us and did not prepare. So we prepared for you. Each village has enough extra food and space to take a few families; hopefully between us we can take all."

His mother stopped talking and sat quietly while Jole tried to absorb her words. He was stunned that the villagers had this knowledge – he needed to see the records as soon as possible.

He was also humbled to know that the villagers, after years of being ignored by the townsfolk, would hold out their hands to help.

Winter in July

It was cold this morning.

First cat woke me up for an early breakfast, his not mine, and I was shivering. I put on an extra layer before going back to bed. It took a while to warm up enough to get back to sleep.

About an hour later I woke again, too cold. I lay there miserably, too tired to get up and too chilled to sleep. Eventually I reached for the laptop and turned it on. Perched on my stomach it heated up quickly (I really must get it fixed). I dozed off.

Second cat came in for a late breakfast. I got up, and started to shiver again within a few minutes.

So I checked the temperature control, just in case it was me not the weather, and then turned the heating on. Only for twenty minutes while my body warmed up. Now I am layered in a warm dress, thick tights, cardigan, slippers and a rug.

It reminds me of the days spent on the farm; no heating, no hot water, just the bitter cold in winter.

I will not be washing my hair today.

I might wash my hands if the water is warm enough?

Listing Now

I made another list today.

Don't you just love the feeling of achievement you get when you write a list? I always make a list when I have too many things to do.

Now I know exactly what I need to do today.

But wait, I missed something. Re-open the file, type in another item, save it, decide it is in the wrong order now (one must be logical) and do a little cutting and pasting. Save the file and close it.

Get a mug of coffee, after all I've made a good start on today's tasks and deserve a break.

Realise the list is too long, I need to prioritise it.

Search for the file; I was sure I'd saved it in an obvious folder. Maybe I should re-organise the folders? But no, I have too much to do today.

Find file, open it, decide which tasks must be done today and highlight them. Then re-order the list so they are at the top. Maybe I should have used a table? Much better than bullets. Set up a table and convert the list. Sort table by priority points.

Realise it's lunchtime, save the file and go into the kitchen.

After lunch and another coffee, I have a short break. I check the TV schedule; there's a programme I really need to watch, and it's on in 15 minutes. No time to start the first priority task so I surf the 'net while waiting.

As the programme ends, a cat appears wanting food; and while in the kitchen I make myself a coffee.

I wonder if I'm drinking too much coffee, and do a search to get the information I'll need to make a decision about whether to drink all of this mug or maybe just half. Wow, there are a lot of sites about caffeine on here. And I didn't know that coffee was grown in Vietnam, I should check that out on some other sites to confirm it.

I pick up my coffee mug; it's empty. And I feel thirsty. I should make some tea, and maybe get a biscuit?

In the kitchen I can't find a clean mug, so I empty the washing up bowl, run hot water and wash a mug. It seems a waste to run the water for so long just for one mug, so I do half the washing up while waiting for the kettle to boil. Then take a clean mug to the kettle; which has grown cold. I re-boil the kettle, make tea, find a biscuit (not that well hidden) and sit down with my drink.

By the time I finish it is getting dark, so I pull the curtains closed, turn on the TV and settle down for the evening.

But eventually all those must-do tasks start to bother me. I search through folders until find the file (why did I save it there?), look at my list. I can't do the first two tasks because they are noisy and it is too late. But I cross off number eight – that was the washing-up and I've done some of that.

I go to bed, so tired and stressed about all the work I have to do.

Always Running

I am running down a long corridor; no doors or windows just the endless blank walls. My legs are aching but still I am running.

After fifteen minutes I see a single arch on my right and I veer off the mental line I've been following into a doorway. Through the door, I slow enough to look around but I don't stop.

I am in a large room, with one door behind me and another ahead. Still no windows but the light is softer and there are benches either side.

Shall I stop? No, the impulse to run is still strong and I run on towards the far doorway.

It takes me into another corridor, so I turn left; continuing the direction of the parallel route I'd been on before.

The brief slower pace has let my lungs refill and I speed up. There are no doorways in sight.

After another ten minutes I see a doorway on my left. The risk that it will just take me back to the other corridor is too high, so I run past.

It was the correct decision as in another five minutes I see a doorway on the right.

Again I enter a large room with a door beyond. As I slow to take in my surroundings I see soft chairs, and even a table on one side. But I do not stop to rest here.

Heading out into the next corridor I turn left again and speed up. In only five minutes I see a door on the left, but I speed past it. Another nine minutes and there is the next doorway on the right. I am still running but I slow before the door this time. Why was the distance only fourteen minutes? What has changed the pattern?

I run past the door and within only a minute there is a second doorway on the right. I turn into the room. Only one door in and one ahead once more, but this time there is a window on my left. I slow enough to look out, but it is a fake view of a garden; I recognise it from yesterday.

Turn left at the door and speed up. I don't bother to count the doors this time, just sprint for fifteen minutes and turn into the doorway.

Another room, another corridor, another room, another corridor. Each room I run through has more things to check, more tables, better chairs, more realistic 'windows'.

At last I enter a room with food on the table. I look around carefully, and then sit and eat. I have finished running for today and can relax. I wash my whiskers and curl up to sleep.

What Do Mermaids Eat?

I am swimming in a cool, sweet-scented lagoon, enjoying the feeling of silky water flowing down my body. My hair streams out behind me, the wetness enhancing the black until it glistens darkly.

Ahead there is a school of small fish, and as I approach them their colours brighten to deep pinks and golds. These anthias are my favourites, they are friendly and happy to escort me around their reef. I slow my strokes and carefully swim into the centre of the school. Then we swim together around to the south side of their reef.

On the way we pass a snapper; he looks at the fish around me hopefully, but a flick of my tail makes him decide to leave my companions alone. I am glad to be of service to my newest friends.

But the time soon comes to move on, and I leave my anthias here as I must swim further south. The northern waters are cooling and I seek a warmer base for the winter.

When I reach the warmer currents I relax and let one of them take me. Then as the current passes near land I rise to the surface and leap from the water, twisting cleanly on the way back down. I re-enter with barely a splash, just enough to make the lone fisherman nervous. Another leap and splash nearer to his boat causes waves that rock his craft and nearly capsize it. He hurriedly packs away his rod and makes for shore.

I smile and wave to the nearest fish, glad they have escaped him for today.

But this encounter means I have to move on further; no good comes of living too near to fishing boats. Not for me or them.

I find another current turning to the south-east, and I float along with it.

After a while I am feeling hungry, but cannot see anything nearby to eat. I swim towards the nearest island.

Here is food, abandoned by my cousins. I surface within the reef and collect the nasty plastic residue before moving to land. By the edge of the water there is a collection box, and the waste I've collected goes in. Then I select a few morsels of better 'left food'. Why do so many humans buy good food and then throw it away? How can they prefer the dead animals smothered in sickly sauces to the fresh taste of lettuce and tomato?

Taking the bounty from the land back to the sea I rinse the last of the sauce from it and crunch down. Lettuce is not much different from some of my usual foods, although less chewy, but tomatoes are the best treat ever.

I think I will settle here for a while.

My Best Enemy

I always found it hard to hate, but somehow you changed that.

My early years where filled with love and caring parents. I was an only one, and all three parents adored me; they complimented my efforts, encouraged me yet set me challenges too. The year I was due to start school they kept me back, worried I was the smallest and youngest and that I might be overlooked or pushed aside. By the second year I'd had a small growth spurt and they happily let me join my year group.

I was advanced in most subjects and at least average in the others so it was a relatively easy transition as far as the learning went. I concentrated on the social aspects and quickly made a couple of friends. The three of us spent every break together, and teamed up in science and sports.

Everything was great until I moved up to the next school. One of my friends' families moved away, and Deawn and I were plunged into the huge maelstrom of the school without them. The school was fed from six schools from the lower level and the resulting noise and confusion would be bad enough to deal with, but that wasn't the main issue. We didn't stand a chance; on the first day the older boys were waiting to pick off the smallest groups and we were chosen immediately.

Even today I cannot remember most of the next two years; they are buried deep. But some of the scenes replay every night in my nightmares.

I am in a corridor, Deawn is behind me. We are creeping quietly along hoping to avoid you, but there you are around the next corner. You loom over me and sweat begins to slide done my arms and legs. You start slowly, a whisper. "And there you are my little friends. I've been worried about you." You smile, but only your lips move, your eyes are hard.

"You should come with me into the staff room, it's nice and quiet there and you'll be safe from the rush."

We follow you silently, what else can we do?

Once in the room all pretence drops. You grab the nearest rod and order Deawn to bend over. "You've been naughty today haven't you. I have to punish you so you'll behave tomorrow."

And so it went on. Once or twice a week for two years.

Until at last the school got a new head-leader, who cancelled the teachers' trips out and stopped them leaving the school in charge of the older pupils at mealtime.

You were still there; still waiting round the corners. But there was always a teacher somewhere behind you, curbing your fun.

Another two years and you were gone; out into the world, leaving Deawn and me to complete our education in peace. But we never forgot.

The day our education finished we drew straws to decide who went first, and I won.

So here I am planning your punishment. I wonder what a suitable revenge is for those two years; what can I do to wipe out our pain?

Shall I come armed with a baton, ready to force you to bend while I beat you? Or take a gun and humiliate you at your workplace? Maybe follow you home and expose you there before forcing you to submit in front of your family? But as I reflect on the punishment I can inflict on you, I realise that I don't need to do any of these. I can punish you without raising an arm. It will take just a few fingers.

I type up my memories, attach a photo of you standing proudly on the steps of the government offices and push 'send'.

I hope Deawn is happy now. Wherever he is.

Flicker

There was a flicker in the corner of my eye.

I barely noticed it; I was listening to a talk about memory, focused on the speaker as she expounded on the way we remember events. The speaker stopped and asked for questions. There was the usual silence, then the man beside me waved his hand. I glanced away as the mic was handed over and he began to speak. It was one of those questions designed to show how much he knew, and the speaker didn't even attempt to respond. As she asked again for questions, with a decided emphasis on the word 'question', I looked back a the podium, and there was another brief flicker on my right.

This time I turned to look, but there was only the group of people I'd spent the day with, and behind them a blank, bland-coloured wall.

I dismissed it, and tried to concentrate on the talk.

I didn't see anything for the rest of the day, and had forgotten it by bedtime.

I slept well.

The next morning, I was up and dressed in plenty of time to stock up on the hotel breakfast. Then, feeling more than a bit over-full I wandered along to the conference room.

And as I sat down, prepared to settle into another interesting session on my favourite topic, I saw a flicker on my left. I turned slowly, but there was just the woman settling into the seat next me. I looked forward again, focusing on the screen.

After a brief video, our speaker spoke for a while about the latest research into sleep and memory. My attention was engaged as she covered the original experiments on dolphins, and the newer work on hummingbirds. I was looking for a new post and this research was recruiting new staff, so I was taking more notes than usual.

But just as she was summarising her session and opening the time up for questions, there was a flicker on my left. And even as I firmly held my head still, another flicker, this time on my right.

I missed the first question; I'd been going to make sure I asked the first one, to make an impression. Now I'd not only missed my chance, but wasn't even sure what had been said.

I was really annoyed. If I asked my rehearsed question now and it was similar to the one I'd, I'd seem stupid so any chance to show off my knowledge was gone.

I didn't stay for the next session. Instead I went up to my room and checked my eyes in the mirror. They seemed fine; no redness and extra lines. I wondered if I was dehydrated – hotels are so dry. I drank two glasses of water and lay on my bed with my eyes shut for a few minutes. Everything was fine. I went back downstairs.

Yet, as I approached the doors to the convention room, there were flickers on both sides, and this time they did not stop. Turning my head made no difference, the flickers at the corners of my field of vision did not stop.

I ran from the hallway, through the hotel until I was outside. At last, as I entered the car park, it stopped.

But only until I looked back towards the hotel, where the windows of the conference rooms were covered with tiny humming birds.

Safety First

I lay by the window, watching the world. Outside the other children played Jump the Road, screaming and laughing when one of them misjudged the jump and fell back. Outside there was no crying, no pain; She took care of that. The excitement was in the skill, not the risk.

But for me there was no skill, and certainly no risk. I lay wrapped in soft cloths, my head firmly supported and my every breath monitored. She would always care for me and keep what little life there was within my body. She would check my nutrient levels, exercise my arms and legs, make sure I felt no pain.

Each day I watched the others play, kept safe yet allowed to stretch their wings. One day it would be jumping, the next perhaps flying. Once I saw them play Dogs and Cats with pretend fights. And always their laughter soared into my room.

She would watch them too, ready to step in should anyone be hurt. She would whisk away the pain and tears as if they'd never happened; all forgotten in an instant caress. And while She watched them, She watched me too. But no caresses for me; my skin was too tender.

For me She tended my cocoon of softness and fed me the drugs and liquid food that kept me alive. The only thing She could not do was make my life worth living. But She could not let me die either.

Revenge is a Dish

He chewed slowly on the last mouthful, feeling pleasantly full. It had been a long time since he'd eaten so well.

After swallowing he looked around regretfully, but not even a crumb was left. "Oh well," he thought, "I have really had sufficient. To want more at the moment would be greedy."

After consoling himself with this, he strolled out and made his way to the river. Sitting on the bank he watched the water flow past, until his eyes closed and he drifted off to sleep.

He dreamed he was chasing a young buck through the forest, cheered on by his father. They ran through dense undergrowth and jumped the streams. But however fast he ran the buck was always a few yards ahead. His heart was racing and his breathing too loud, but still they ran. At last he began to close the gap and anticipation of the win gave him extra speed. Then, at the last moment his father pushed ahead of him and brought the buck down.

"Too slow my lad," he laughed, and picking up the prize he strode off leaving the youth behind.

This was enough to rouse him to the present, feeling the discomfort of an over-full stomach, mixed with the pain and anger of the memory.

"He never let me win, not even once. He always had to be first. Then he complained when I gave up competing. What did he expect!"

Rolling onto his side he tried to block these painful thoughts. After all, he had won in the end. He had beaten his father in the best possible way.

When his first book was published, he'd dedicated it to 'My father, without whom I would have remained just one of the herd'; a less than subtle dig at his father's bullying and shouting skills. Yes, his delight in publishing the first vegan recipe book was from the victory he'd got by challenging the very core of his father's reputation, as much as his delight in the acclaim from his peers.

He rumbled contentedly, with just a wisp of smoke. His first book 'Vegan Cooking for Dragons' had achieved all he'd ever wanted – his father's humiliation.

Fourteen Minus One
For Zander, who inspired it

The house, quiet for many weeks, began to stir. Dust swirled gently and the cobwebs swayed, as if someone had walked past quietly.

As the night drew in, there was rustling and the sound of thousands of tiny feet; followed by a mass exodus of mice. They ran from the house as if a fire drove them, as if the house rejected them, preparing for its real tenants.

There was a rumbling sound; the house was waking. Lights shone from the windows and soft music played.

There was a moment of stillness; then the dust swirled madly, forming the shapes of people long gone. They coalesced into arms, legs, the beginnings of bodies, and then collapsed. The dust moved faster, as if trying to build the shapes before they fell. Faces appeared, gaping, staring, holding for minutes then melting away.

The mad, distorted figures danced; at first alone, then forming into couples. They were becoming clearer as the music bound them.

The front door opened and a cold wind blew in, bringing down dust from the curtains into the dance.

Then the house sighed – at last there were exactly six couples; twelve dust shapes created on this special night.

Twelve dancers to share a house with its owner.

The house was content. Its door closed softly, the number 13 shining out into the night.

Give Me Three Words and I Will Tell a Story

I used to tell children's stories based on two or three words. "Just give me a name and a place and I'll start."

When I started writing my stories down instead I'd sometimes ask friends for some words; names, nouns, verbs, anything.

This next section has some of the tales based on prompts from friends on Facebook, Dreamwidth and Livejournal, and from Bec (a colleague on the Admissions Appeals Panel).

That Thing
Mary Ward: Baby; trees; pot

The bundle cried.
He looked in disgust.
Why would anyone want this
squalling smelly thing?

They said it would grow,
but he'd measured it every day
and it was still too small;
too small, too noisy.

Mother fed it often.
Even when it was his dinnertime
that thing was fed first
and he had to wait.

Maybe she fed it wrong?
Just milk wasn't enough?
He looked in the cupboards
for better food.

Amazing Growth!!
He spelt out the word,
looked it up to check.
This was good for growing.

Dad used it for the baby trees
so they would make a huge hedge,
spreading quickly
over the broken fence.

He found a pot and the peat
and copying his dad
planted the baby
in Amazing Growth!!

Cat, Butterfly, Dragon
Peggi Warner-Lalonde: Cat; butterfly; dragon

I stretched lazily, my fur warm from the morning sun; paused to consider if I was hungry, but decided to take a gentle stroll first. Just around the garden, enough to wake me up. Then I would call the Big Her and have my bowl refilled.

I love snacking in the morning after a light nap, before I return to lie on the hot stones and relax.

I set off towards the back hedge; not hunting, but knowing I would consider it if anything interesting appeared. From the back I circled towards the 'flowers'. Big Her doesn't like me digging here, but the ground was soft and tempting.

A pause ...

I cleaned myself and resumed my perambulation. a slow majestic march.

Then I saw it, one of those fluttering things. They are such fun to chase. Some more than others, but all great fun, even if if I couldn't eat them.

This one was flapping towards the flowers ahead of me, and suddenly my other self took over. I ran towards the flowers, then crouched and waited. It didn't even notice me! As it settled on a tall flower in front of me I jumped, claws out. A perfect 10! A clean catch, and here it was struggling between my paws. I transferred it to my mouth, trying to ignore the nasty powdery taste, and carried it over to my favourite sleeping spot.

But halfway there, the fluttery prey stung me! How could it do that? These 'butterflats' usually died easily, too easily really, but this?

Again the flare of pain in my mouth. I spat out the thing. And looking carefully I could see now that it was not a flutterfly. The sun glinted off the tips of the wings, and its open mouth revealed teeth. There was a flare of heat, like the flame Big Her makes to light the tubes, and part of my whiskers curled into black ash.

I backed away, waiting for movement. But it just sat where I'd dropped it, staring at me.

I moved forward and stretched a paw to tap it. Again the flare, and my toes hurt. A stabbing pain.

I retreated to lick my wounds. It sat watching. My other self was demanding I fight and conquer, but I did not understand this thing. It flew, like many of my prey, but unlike them it fought back.

The waiting seemed endless.

At last Big Her came out to see what I was doing. She looked at the flyer and exclaimed "Why that's a dragon toy! Where on earth did you get it puss?" She picked it up and tossed it into the hedge.

A dragon! I remember mother telling us kits about the days of old and the old enemies. There used to be dragons, but mother said they were gone.

I walked away proudly.

I am a cat scientist. I have found the long-lost dragons.

A Nice Dress
Sam Mason: nice; pink; dress

"We'll need to get you a dress for the wedding," announced mother as she walked into my bedroom without knocking.

"You didn't knock! Again!" I protested. Then her words sank in. A dress. She expected me to wear a dress.

"I don't need a dress," I said "I already have my interview suit, that will do."

"I'm not having you go to a wedding in that suit. Not this time. You'll behave like a proper girl and wear a pretty dress like the other girls. I am not going to let you show me up again in front of the family and my friends." And with that she turned and walked out, ignoring my protests.

I turned down the music and lay back on the bed. Why did she keep trying to mould me into my sister? Why couldn't she just accept me?

I logged into Headwrite and typed in an angry message for my friends; at least they would understand how I felt. Within a couple of minutes I had three replies.

Sara agreed with me, but she always does. Sara doesn't do conflict.

Jilly was more analytical, and wanted to know why my mother wanted me in a dress; and more questions about why I never wore dresses.

And then there was Tom. He actually wrote that I would look good in a dress because I had 'nice' legs.

I clicked 'love it' on Sara's post, deleted Tom from my pals list and started to type a reply for Jilly.

"I hate wearing dresses. I was forced to wear a dress for primary school, but once I moved up I got some smart black trousers instead. My mother kept trying to get me into a 'nice dress', but I'd wear them to climb trees or when I was fishing. I'd come with filthy marks and torn hems on them every time, until she gave up.

"I look good in trousers and I like wearing them. And I bought myself a smart trouser suit with my Christmas money last year. So why should I wear a dress!"

Jilly posted back:
"OK, but this seems to be really important to your mum. Can't you compromise just this once?"

But it won't be just once. If I give in, Mother will resume her endless quest to turn me into a girly girl. She'll nag and try to persuade; she'll bargain and promise me treats. And eventually I'll have to move out to escape it all.

I've been saving up to move into my own place, but I don't have enough yet. Also, apart from the issues over my choice of clothes, we got on well most of the time. I hoped we could get past this, although it won't be because I compromise over wearing a dress.

Mother waited until I was dressed then called me down.

"We are going shopping right now. No arguments. You are going to try on some dresses. If you can convince me you don't look pretty in them, I will let you try on something else, but you have to try the dresses first."

She drove us to the mall, and dragged me into one of the teenage girls' shops. In there she selected an armful of pastel coloured summer dresses and thrust them at me. "Try these! I want to see them on you."

I turned my back on the mirror in the changing room and pulled one of the dresses on at random. It was frilly and had lots of bows on it. I felt like throwing up.

As soon as I appeared at the door Mother gushed and cooed in a sickening way.

"Oh you look so pretty, that colour really suits you," she exclaimed.

I knew at that moment I had lost. She was never going to give in. I would be wearing a nice, pink dress to her wedding.

And for those who like dresses
A Nice Dress Too

I wanted a new dress for the summer as my old ones were looking somewhat battered. One had worn out along the seams and was in danger of splitting open in the wash.

I searched online for a dress. Not too many requirements. I wanted a long dress. It needed to have sleeves. And at least part cotton or other natural material.

Oh, and in my size.

Unfortunately most clothes shops don't sell stuff in my size, and the ones that do can be too expensive. But there are some shops I can find clothes in that fit me and that I like.

But not dresses. Not this year. I appear to be out of fashion again.

There are plenty of dresses, sleeveless, in sticky hot plastics. But nothing cool and affordable.

I try the auction sites, but in no time my filters reduce the thousands of dresses to a few hundred; and most of those in colours and patterns I don't like. Still I click on one.

It is nylon.

Why do sellers do this? It only takes a minute to use the correct word!
I scroll down, ignoring the obvious errors (since when were maxi dresses above the knee?). I click on every likely candidate for over 30 minutes. Then I give up.

Two days later. I still need at least one summer dress so I start again.

Three hours later I give up again.

A week goes by and one of my remaining dresses goes in the recycling bin.

I search again. Through the sites that sell clothes in 'PLUS' sizes, then back onto the auction sites.

And through the thousands of 'unspecified' listings (don't they want to sell their clothes?).

At last, after several hours and several mugs of coffee, I find one dress. In my size, with short sleeves, part cotton.

It is in a colour I rarely wear, but this year I will. I click on 'buy' and quickly pay for it before it disappears.

This year I will be wearing a nice, pink dress!

Conversations
"elaiel": bride; touch; folly

It was time to think about retiring.

He was looking forward to having enough time to create the garden he'd dreamed about for years. It would have fruit trees and a herb garden, with space for a greenhouse and a shed for his tools.

She wanted to move somewhere warm, where she could spend hours lying in a hammock, sipping wine and relaxing. They would have a maid to do the housework.

They had not talked to each other about the future.

It was only a few weeks before he retired.

His office sent him on a 'preparing for retirement' workshop. He worked through the figures with the workshop leader, and finally accepted that his dream was too expensive. He was depressed.

She would be retiring a month later.

She started cleaning out the cupboards ready to move. She couldn't wait to get out of this tiny flat, built over a noisy street and full of dust.

One evening the TV stopped working.

They sat in the living room, wondering who would break the uncomfortable silence. Finally he spoke. "I see you've been having a clear out."

"Well I thought one of us should make a start, there's not much time left before we are free." And she smiled tentatively at him.

There was another silence.

"Yes, well I've been thinking. Maybe I should stay on a bit longer? After all, lots of people retire later these days."

Her smile froze. "But we planned! We always said we would retire to the south coast!"

"I know, but that was when the children were little; we planned a lot of things then, but we never did them."

"Well obviously having children changed things but that was then. We never said we wouldn't retire, just as we always wanted!" She was getting angry now, all her hopes, all those dreams that made her endless days at work bearable and he just expected her to accept he wanted something different.

He began to wish he'd not spoken. How could he explain his failure?

"I am sorry. I just didn't know how to tell you. I thought we'd have enough money with our pensions and the sale of the flat. But property prices here are low and places on the coast are now much more expensive. We just can't afford to buy anything there, not even a flat." He couldn't look at her as he broke the devastating news.

"Oh Jim, why didn't you tell me sooner. We need to talk to each other more!" and she laughed. "I've been saving for our move for years. I started saving for our girl's wedding when she was little; we both wanted her to have a perfect wedding and she did make a beautiful bride. Then after I just left the direct debit going. I checked the account a couple of weeks ago, and I am sure we can get a place. It may not be quite what we wanted, but it will be near the coast and have a garden."

And for the first time in months they smiled at each other. He reached out to touch her hand, and suddenly they were hugging and smiling as if they'd never drifted apart.

"I've been foolish," he muttered.

"We've both been a bit foolish," she replied. Then she remembered. She turned to pick up the property listings she been studying. There it was -an old folly for sale. It needed work, so was priced much lower than the comfortable new bungalows on the opposite page, but they were still fit enough to take on a project.

And there were two perfect pairs of trees in the side garden just right for hammocks; the maid could wait.

If Only
Bec Cope: appeal; Miranda; disappointed

He'd seen her on the bus several times, and he'd noticed that she always seemed cheerful. She smiled at the driver when he handed her a ticket. She smiled at the woman in the seat next to her. She even smiled at him when he stood back to let her get off the bus first.

But he was too scared to speak to her.

He knew that his skinny frame and acne didn't appeal to girls. If he ever forgot for a few minutes, he only had to remember Miranda from school and how she had ridiculed him in front of everyone when he'd asked her to dance at the prom.

So rather than risk humiliation and be disappointed again, he just watched as she walked away.

NaNoWriMo Challenge:
50 Words About Childhood

"I'll go first," she whispered. "Follow me."

We scanned the corridor; she nudged the door while I tried to silence my breathing.

The room was empty; we crept in; she grabbed them.

Resisting the urge to run, we crept out.

Her hand opened, revealing chocolates stolen from her parents.

Almost Non-Fiction

The What Do You Call It?

I marched into the doing room and looked for the gizmo. Finally found it under a squishy thingy.

I zapped the picture maker. Nothing interesting on there. One day I might try to find out how the woman next door gets that series that I like on hers.

The sit-on block was comfy, so I didn't feel like going round to visit whatsername just yet. I could always watch my favourite series later.

But I was feeling hungry, or maybe I was just thirsty? I wanted a drink of something. I walked into the cooking room and looked at the thingamajigs I have to press.

Hmmm. Ta, Coffee, Chocolate?

It seemed the doohicky marked 'ta' was the most used, so I pressed it. Out came a whatsit, then some dark stuff, followed by white stuff. I took it up carefully and sipped. It tasted OK.

I carried the thingumabob containing the 'ta' back to the doing room and sat on the whatchamacallit. Nearby was the gadget I'd been fixing yesterday. I picked up the thingummy I needed to fix the bits back inside.

Then, my brain exhausted by all the thinking, I went back to the lay-down-on-oojah.

Venturing Out

I leave my cave several times a week to forage. The journey can be difficult, but so far I have survived.

On leaving my cave today I joined a small trail. Alongside is a deeper, wider trail, carved by the hard shells used by the stronger hunters. It was strange to see how the hunters use their shells, leaving them at night to enter their caves, but my mother explained how some crabs use shells they can take over, then leave behind, and that some tribes had adopted the idea.

I try to stay on the small trail, as hunters who use shells are not always friendly. Several of the tribe had encountered them on the deep trails and suffered.

The first steps are easy, but as I turn onto the trail I see obstacles ahead. The hunters have left their shells across my path again. This means I must detour onto the deep trail, making sure none of the shells are moving. My heart beats fast as I check that the shells are empty; twice recently I have edged around a shell blocking the trail only to have the hunter inside come at me – the sight of a shell bearing down is truly terrifying.

I escaped the attacks, but would not want to risk it again.

After this, the trail is usually clear for a way but, at the point where I must turn again onto a side trail, there are more tests. Part of the trail is overgrown, as the jungle tries to reclaim it. The first outgrowth has sharp points, and today I have left my gauntlets behind. Do I push past and risk cuts, or again step into the shell path? Today I use my pouch to push the points aside. The pouch is scored but my skin is safe.

Further down other growths stretch almost fully across the trail. Although these have no points, the trail is closed and I must step down. I am lucky and there are no shells moving, so I stride out and round the growths safely.

Just ahead I join a main trail; it is clear and wide so I can stay on the trail without danger. Once again I have survived the journey.

(I'd been annoyed enough to be at least a little tempted to 'key' all the cars and overgrown bushes blocking the pavements on my walk from home to work that day, but then wrote this instead.)

Why Has the Toaster Played Such an Important Role in Weddings?

It is no accident that the recent decline in the custom of giving multiple electric toasters at weddings occurred at the same time as the rate of divorce increased dramatically. What has been forgotten somewhere in the mists of time is why the toaster has had such a prominent role in binding couples together.

According to my research the humble toaster evolved over centuries from a basic burning of the bread ceremony found in many western cultures.

The significance of grains in harvest and fertility customs

Because the first farmers saw their seeds sprout and grow quickly, grain became a potent symbol of fertility. In the north of Wash, fathers were paid in bags of grain for their sons, and the couples were showered with grains (although this was usually grass seed as it was plentiful and cheap).

Why heating grains increase their potency

Grain can be either 'popped', as in the far west, or baked. Baking was the preferred method across much of Europe. The ritual of pushing and pulling the wet mixture and then watching the miracle of it swelling was the perfect link to the growing of both crops and animals. So it was inevitable that bread, rising in the heat would take on an even stronger symbolic role in people's lives. And the women who made good bread became famed across the country.

With the development of sweet breads made with honey and fruits, the women who passed on these secret recipes through their daughters, held power over the village, and especially because it was believed that their contribution to the wedding feast ensured a fertile union.

Some of the eastern tribes in the Angleia believe to this day that bread, or cake if rich enough, should form the centre piece of the wedding meal.

Early toasting appliances, and the place of the blacksmith

As civilisation moved on, and possibly upwards, households demanded more gadgets. One of the first, and the most popular, was the toasting fork. This replaced the ordinary forks that had led to several unfortunate incidents. Soon, no household worth its salt was without a toasting fork, and local blacksmiths were overwhelmed with the demand during the marriage season.

This appears to be the reason that inviting a blacksmith (confused in later times with chimney sweeps) was considered lucky.

Introducing high tech, the decline in female/rural power

Once industrialisation overtook the simple smithy, the toasting fork was upgraded to the toaster or grill. (I have read that it was the popularity of the grill section that led to the huge sales of the modern 'cooker'.) Later, yet again, it was the humble but so important new stand-alone toaster that started the avalanche of small electrified household goods. Even in the tiniest kitchen, it became the norm to have at least nine of these in the first year (nine being a very special number of course).

However, the unfortunate side effect was to increase the move from the bread as a local, rural product into a mass-produced objects toasted in yet more massed produced objects. The skill of the bread-maker and the household toast-woman was no longer revered.

For a while the old customs persisted, and any new household was assured of a plentiful supply of toasters. But inevitably over time people forgot why they did this, and the giving of toasters declined.

And with it, the magic that supported the longevity of the marriage bond died too.

An Endless Circle

Benji

Stretched out on the cushion, enjoying a digestive midday nap, I suddenly hear the sound of the catflap.

There is a soft thud, then silence. Next the sounds of someone eating; chewing, licking, the sounds of someone at my food bowl.

I wait, tail twitching but otherwise still. The food bowl is too near the back door and I want the intruder to come further into my home.

His head appears around the doorway. He walks confidently into my living room, lulled by the lack of any attack as he stole my food.

I sniff the air, no familiar smells; he does not belong here.

As soon as he clears the door and is in the most exposed space I jump; my claws out, my teeth ready.

I land next to him, lunging forward to grab his neck; revelling in his scream of fear.

"Stop it Benji!" she shouts. She rises from the chair and chases me away from this trespasser. Then she bends towards him speaking softly. "Poor Bilbo, did your brother hurt you?" She pets him carefully, then strokes him.

Finally she turns to me. "Bad Benji!" she says firmly.

I look at her in dismay; why has she welcomed this stranger into our home? He smells of dog and man and other cats. He does not live here.

Bilbo

I've been visiting one of my friends. He likes me to visit him and I love his comfy lap and warm house. But now it is time to go home.

I have a quick check of the food bowls on the way in, and lick up the remnants of breakfast. Then into the living room to find a soft spot for my next nap.

I've padding across the room to check on her, when suddenly I am hit by the thud of a heavy body and pain in my neck. I cry out from the shock. He is holding me down, claws digging in and I struggle to escape; trying to get out of the house that should be my comfort.

She intervenes, tries to calm me down but I don't want to stay here now.

I'll go back to my new friend, and return later - hoping by then that my brother will have calmed down.

They knew they had the answer

The physicists spoke in lofty halls, declaiming their conclusions, speaking with conviction. There was no room for doubt, and lately no room for new information to add to the knowledge. This was The Theory and it was finished.

Until a quiet voice spoke up. A question carefully phrased, wrapped in praise and lightly touched on.

They reacted angrily, forgetting their own past. How dare he speak. How dare he suggest they might have missed something, even something so small. He was wrong. They took turns attacking him with words until he subsided.

A few days later there was a sentence in the report of the proceedings. His quiet question repeated. They wrote letters full of condescension-covered hate.

A year later some research was published. They decried the science, ridiculed the authors. But the journal refused to retract the article.

Another team replicated the research, and published. This time when They tried ridicule a few others spoke against them. This was unheard of! They were the experts, revered by all, how dare others put them down. Some people did not get grants that year.

By the fourth year They retreated, still convinced they were right but the opposition was too strong. All those young idiots following a fad.

And then his small idea grew and Their idea was left to the history books.

He was excited; full of enthusiasm. He welcomed others in to share his delight in the new idea. They talked late into the nights talking and bouncing the new models around until it was hard to remember who first spoke each added development.

They had the theory, in its full glory. Thus a new theory crystallised.

But new research removed the foundations, Quantum tunnelling was the way forward.

Meanwhile, in another room at another conference, a biologist described the journey to their final theory of our life. They had fitted Lucy into the line and the line had few gaps. There was no doubt that homo sapiens had emerged by tiny steps from these ancestors. There was a little work to be done to fill in a few gaps, but the overall story was written.

This time there were no small questions, instead there was DNA, and new bones. The single line ascending from the past was tangled up in new information. Confronting a simple message with complexity.

This is a story about people who start fresh with curiosity and spirit but who grow around their ideas until the idea is fixed within them. They achieve respect, and power, and misuse this to protect their babies. They reject Truth as strongly as they embraced it before.

And science, even though some scientists avoid it, science is the poorer for this.

And when the space craft come, and we face greater challenges to our ideas, our theories and our beliefs – will we deny them?

Life, Facts and Thoughts

Myths and Science - The Impact of the Observer

Today my sister posted an old 'fact' about cheetahs, pointing out again that it had been disproved by real research and real numbers. It was disproved many years ago, but the false information continues to spread down each generation, so much faster than the truth.

It reminded me about one of my favourite stories. There are plenty of examples of researchers misusing statistics: too few test subjects, the wrong analysis; too much data mining; etc. But this one is a little different.

I was on the behaviour module of my biology degree, and the Head of Biological Sciences took us to watch pairs of mice in large cages.

We 'observed' their mating behaviour before they were together and during the preliminary 'courtship'.

It was clear to us that both the female and male mice were involved in active mating behaviour.

Then he told us that, until the mid 1970s, all the observers described male mouse activity reasonably accurately but female mice were described merely as 'receptive' (i.e. the females just sat there, then they would passively let the male mount). It was only with the start of 'feminist biology' that the accounts of the activity of the females included observations of them engaging in 'lordosis' and other proceptive behaviour. In fact (as the facts are understood now) females often initiate mating.

There appear to be two possible explanations:
female mice were affected by human feminists and suddenly became proactive; or

the observers' expectations and cultural influences blinded them to this behaviour, as they believed it did not exist in females.

A great example of why you should never just accept research into behaviour when it relies on human interpretation.

There are so many other examples from USA behavioural and observational scientists in the 20th century. Many of these are embedded in books and referenced in other papers. The amended or corrected analyses make take years to spread through the scientific community, and even longer to drip into the media and society.

So take your observational science with a pinch of salt, because there is no such thing as an unbiased, strictly logical observer.

Not Learning to Drive

I never learnt to drive. I'd planned to but life intervened.

I got my shiny new provisional licence when I was 18. I had a couple of attempts in a boyfriend's car on the old aerodrome and planned to pay for real lessons when I got a proper job.

I left school, and worked shifts in a factory for a few weeks. Then the letter offering me an interview for that 'proper' job arrived. I passed the interview, was asked to do some extra tests and there I was about to become a computer programmer.

Just one small thing to get through first – a medical with my local Medical Officer for Health. No problem, I was fit and healthy.

But it didn't quite work out. He was most of the way through the tests and examinations when he checked my eyes. And failed me.

I couldn't believe it. I knew I had a sight problem, but everyone had mostly ignored it. There were the annual visits to the eye department at Salisbury hospital, and glasses prescribed when I was 13 or 14, but no one had ever suggested I couldn't work in an office because of it.

I protested to the doctor; after all I'd just left school armed with A levels – so obviously there wasn't an issue reading papers and writing.

Finally he relented, and passed me fit for work.

And then told me I mustn't drive. And ordered me to return my licence to the Driver Licensing Agency.

I left his office, pleased about the fact that I still had a job, but stunned by the fact that I'd never be allowed to drive a car or bike.

Many years later I discovered he was wrong, I could have been a driver, but too late now.

A TWO HUNDRED PER CENT INCREASE!!

Yes indeed readers, we have a 200 per cent increase in ...

Or was it merely a 150 per cent increase?

Well, if you know anything about numbers and fractions, no. It wasn't. It can't be.

Imagine a large chocolate cake; my son's favourite tool for learning maths as a toddler. You have four people waiting to eat it, and they all want a fair share ... or more. So you carefully cut the cake into four pieces, all the same size. You have four quarters, right?

And a quarter of a hundred is 25%. So each person gets 25 per cent of the cake.

So far this seems to be very basic. So how did we get from a circle cut into four sections, 4 quarters, each 25 per cent of the whole, to a 200 per cent cake?

Imaginary effort
Giving a hundred per cent used to mean giving everything you could, your maximum effort. But over time this didn't sound enough; after all, anyone could give a 100 per cent. So the hyperbolic '110%' crept in to the language. We all knew it wasn't real, but it sounded good. All that extra effort needed some exaggeration.

Then there was inflation. If everyone else was now giving 110 per cent, it wasn't enough for our team; 'We' were going to give '150%'.

Imaginary extra cake?
So far, we had real numbers and we had the sales pitch. But over time they merged and people forgot that 110 per cent isn't real. So now we have parts of a chocolate cake that are bigger than the whole cake.

The inflation of the hyperbole grew, and even 150 per cent wasn't enough: we needed to do '200%' just to keep pace with the old 100 per cent effort.

And so now we apparently have increases of 200 per cent as well. Or even decreases of 100 per cent, in an alternative universe where you still have cake after taking 100 slices away from a 100 piece cake.

Back to reality
But all that cute % sign means is that we have fractions of the cake, from a chocolate cake big enough to serve to 100 people.

There is no way we can serve 200 slices, each one measuring one hundredth of the cake. At least not in this universe.

Things get bigger, smaller, prices increase, more people are unemployed, chocolate bars shrink, but at the end they can all only be 100 per cent of themselves.

Flying Home the Long Way

I had a somewhat strange trip home on Wednesday.

We were flying from Manchester to London City airport – the plane left a bit late but made up the time.

The flight was smooth and we had calm weather. Then there was a message from the Captain to say we would be landing in about 10 minutes (slightly early). A few minutes later the seat belt signs go on, and cabin crew quickly clear the glasses and plates.

Then we carry on flying .... and after a while I realised I'd already seen the lights below .... and there they are again ....

We circled at least four times; then we turned and circled in the opposite direction.

Eventually, some 25 minutes after the announcement, we start descending. We land and trundle down the runway, then stop ....
Captain informs us we are waiting for a gate slot ....

We finally move up nearer to the building, by now at least 20 minutes late instead of early as promised. Then we wait again.

At City airport, which is small, one usually gets off and walks across the tarmac, but it emerged - our Captain was being very quiet by now - that we were waiting for a shuttle bus.

So we finally get off, climb onto the coach and it drives off ....

into a tight circle, to come up behind a coach at a gate a few metres behind our starting point. Our driver stops, waits, gets off to speak to someone, gets back into his seat then pulls out past the coach into a tight figure of eight (i.e. past the coach, round behind it again then off in the opposite direction a few metres).

We wait again.

We are now less than double the usual distance I would have to walk from the plane to a gate and not far from our plane.

And they finally let us out to walk into the building.

Presumably someone thought we would get so dizzy from all the circling that we wouldn't realise we'd been put on a coach to use up more time while waiting for a gate?

Warning, Invisible Monsters in the Dysk!!!
(Written for the 2012 UK Discworld Convention)

Amidst the bustle of the Con, you may be forgiven for not noticing us. No doubt you will have your eyes, and ears, fixed on the Guests of Honour, or the fantastic costumes or be rushing to get a drink (see grump below).

But you'll eventually notice some of us ...

We are the secret legion of disabled fandom. We are the people walking too slowly in the corridors or, even worse, we're wheeling vicious contraptions below eye height, waiting for a chance to crush your toes.

So first let me introduce you to Beaker

It's a lightweight mobility scooter. No flashing lights, no noisy bell, but it gives me the freedom to join you at DWCon.

Well, that's the theory.

The reality is that navigating corridors full of enthusiastic fans can be my worst nightmare (OK, maybe not the worst one, but close). In spite of driving a vicious monster who could leave you with bruises and very sore feet, somehow Beaker and I are invisible.

So, if we are all going to have a good time that doesn't include accidents, frustration or any other unpleasantness, I have a few suggestions.

People with disabilities/disabled people (please select the current acceptable form) find conventions tiring. Most of us appreciate a helping hand.

Rule 1
Ask us, don't assume.

Suddenly pushing someone from behind is scary and dangerous.

And yanking open doors when we are carefully balanced with a hand on the door leads to bad accidents (as the tech crew at another con discovered when someone did it to me).

On the other hand, wheelchairs do not like carpets. It's very hard work wheeling around hotel corridors and some of us might want the occasional push while the arms recover.
As for those heavy doors!

Next
OK, that's the easy bit. You haven't stepped backwards without checking for us, or small children, and you rescued that hot drink I was trying to carry with my third hand.

But I'm riding a scooter, so you are more likely to notice me: who else did you miss?

The Blue Dots

You may not realise they are there; not all of us have pet monsters to convey us through the crowded halls.
BUT, we can be identified by the small dots of blue on our badges.

And the fact that those little blue dots mean we get into the main con rooms first.

Not just because we feel we sometimes deserve a little extra, but because it is safer. We can take our time getting in and finding suitable seats without anyone tripping over us.

(And, if you have never tried walking sideways down a row of seats with crutches or a walking stick, we'll be happy to show you why it doesn't work.)

But Why is She Wearing a Blue Dot?
(Where are the really Invisible Monsters?)

You've just seen someone in the fast-track queue. But they aren't in a wheelchair, or using a walking stick, and they don't have a white cane.

If you are a tabloid media reader in the UK, you might assume they are faking a disability to get a good seat.

But there are hundreds of disabilities that you can't see without blood tests, scans, etc.
And many invisible illnesses cause pain and exhaustion, and many treatments cause weight gain. Some of us have good days (or a few minutes of good) when we might walk the halls, followed later by pain and collapse - so give us the benefit of the doubt and offer help.

But He Didn't Answer Me!

Umm, tricky one – maybe he only speaks KLINGON.

Maybe he's too busy staying upright.
Or, just maybe, he's had a bad day and feels grumpy.
Oh, and did you check for a hearing aid?

Please Don't Give Up
Some of us welcome help, some find it a reminder of their lost independence or are still adjusting.
And remember we are fans too, rushing to get in the queues for food, drink and Him - and looking at costumes.

Summary
Blue dots = be careful, don't rush, please offer help.
Useful help = opening doors (check first), offering to push, carrying hot things, giving way in the corridors, getting up from the comfy chair ... but mainly BEING AWARE.
And talking to us!

And Us?
Be polite when you're offered help – decline politely if you don't need/want it, but explain why. Otherwise the rest of us might be a bit fed up when no one offers to help any of us.

The Grump
This hotel removed the ramp at the nearest end of the bar area during their last renovation/'upgrade', so even if we got a head start we would always end up at the back of the bar queue; below the height of the bar and unseen by the staff.

Moar Invisible Monsters
(Sharing space with others part II)

Many generations ago, in round world, people thought that diseases were caused by miasmas. Then more science was invented and such ideas ridiculed.

But they are wrong. Some of us are badly affected even today by miasmas. They lurk in corridors, in rooms, around the bar. They've even been known to follow us into lunch, wrecking our appetites.

How do you know if a con member is being attacked by a miasma?

There are clear symptoms of a miasmal attack.

Depending on the type (of con member) -
They may be coughing and making unpleasant breathing noises. In a bad case, they may actually breathe so loud they ruin the GoH slots.
Others may suddenly turn a startling colour - you can see the red blotches creeping across their faces.
Or someone might have strange lumps on their skin, breaking out in seconds.

These interruptions to your weekend are a nuisance, so we recommend you do what you can to avoid assisting the miasmas to catch any one here.

Do
Avoid excessive smelly products where possible. Cold water is perfectly adequate for removing ageing natural smells before they become offensive. If you cannot stand under a cold shower, warm water and soap will do.

Granny had some excellent advice about this.

Do Not
Ever, ever, EVER, spray hair products in communal areas. Yes this does mean the Water Closets. (I think Granny was right here, having the unmentionable inside the house is so unhealthy).

Use large amounts of unguents.

Smoke any herbs in the doorways.

If
You have smelly items that are needed to keep your own miasmas and tiny animals away, then please be careful that you are not accidentally poisoning the other fans around you.

Thank you all.

Dancing in the Forests of My Mind

When I was young I loved to dance in the bluebell woods. The music played in my head as I waltzed and spun and leapt. I danced in the sunlight. I danced in cool spring rain. I loved to dance.

I danced among the trees, feeling part of the forests; the branches waving in time to the music I followed.

Then I learned to dance as others did, to music from bands and the radio. I learned to twirl and bend as I held on to others. I danced in darkened halls at weekends. And in my room, and in the garden on dark nights. I always danced.

In my twenties I danced with my babies, to lullabies and playgroup songs. And when they slept I still danced in the bluebell woods in my mind; the music and the memories of scents and gentle breezes so clear. Yes, in my mind I danced.

Then the enemy attacked; and my body started fighting against me. For a while I still danced, but as my joints rebelled and stiffened the pain would overtake the pleasure. Music became bitter-sweet as every song still resonated with leaps and turns instead my head. I stopped listening to music during the day. But I couldn't avoid it completely.

When I heard the melodies I still danced inside my mind. And often I wanted to cry.

Then another change.

I used to sing sometimes, although it was not my first love. And so I began to sing again, and gradually the melodies transformed, from steps my body could not follow to harmonies, to words and sounds.

Now I sing.

But sometimes, in my mind, I dance.

Real Milk

I took the large jug, and walked carefully out of the house and along the path to the milking parlour.

Inside it was always warm, and filled with the scents of clean straw, cows and milk. Still holding the jug with care I approached him. "We need some milk, please."

He carried on milking the cow, and I stood watching his hands on the cow's udders, pulling down so strong and confidently as the milk gushed into the pail. When the flow slowed to a trickle he moved back, patted the cow on the rump, muttered, "Alright girl" to her, and finally looked up and spoke to me.

"Follow me."

We walked the short distance to the cooler – a large, tall, metal container attached to a water pipe. The cold water ran through the inside tunnels, while the milk cascaded down over it and into a large milk churn.

He took the kitchen jug and held it under the flow until it was full of cool frothy milk, then passed it to me. "There you are girl, be careful". I carried it with both hands, walking back to the kitchen as if I was walking a tightrope..

Sitting at the table again, I received a glass full of creamy cool milk, the reward for my efforts.

Winter in July

1. This morning it was colder than normal for the time of year.

2. A cat woke me up.

3. I got up, and then fed the cat.

4. I felt too cold so I put on an extra layer of clothing before going back to bed.

5. It took a while to become warm enough to get back to sleep.

6. 58 minutes later I woke again, feeling cold.

7. I was too cold to sleep.

8. I felt too tired to get up and too chilled to sleep. A conundrum.

9. After 9 minutes trying to sleep, I reached for the laptop and turned it on.

10. I put it on my stomach.

11. It heated up quickly.

13. I got up, and started to shiver again in a few minutes.

14. I turned the heating on.

15. The house is too cold for me to even wash my hair today.

I Struggled to Learn to Read

In an age when dyslexia didn't exist, at least according to the Teaching Unions in the UK, my learning disability was ignored. After all I could talk – a lot – and told stories.

At school I was 'too shy', 'too quiet' and, sometimes, 'lazy'.

I was one of the lucky ones; for a couple of terms we went to a small private school and the headmistress taught me to read my first book. I would stand next to her desk as we tried to get the blocks of black ink to transform into words. And one day there it was – the word 'goat' standing out on a page amidst strings of complex, random shapes.

I have a wide vocabulary, but the lists of words I can read and the words I can speak are not the same. I sometimes describe unknown words on a page as 'standing out as if they are Chinese symbols in the middle of a page of text'. And as for speaking them aloud – I have to hear someone else say them for me first. And not just once.

The list of words I can spell is much shorter. This is why for many years I was a storyteller who never wrote my stories down, until a miracle happened and someone developed a recording device and then, even better, a spellchecker.

But spellcheckers are not always my friends. How did Members' become Bessemers in the text I sent the other day?

Bread and Butter

I kneel on the floor, large bowl in front of me, sleeves rolled up.

A pause to gather my breath, and then I bend over the bowl. Using my weight, through my shoulders, I begin to punch into the dough. It resists at first, but gradually comes together in a uniform ball. I stretch it, then roll, then punch; repeating this over and over until its texture is smooth and supple.

Then a damp teacloth to cover and a warm place to wait.

The smell of yeast begins to drift from the cupboard; not the irresistible smell of bread yet, but the sign that the miracle will be ready to view soon.

I wait, learning patience.

At last it is time to check on progress. The teacloth is still flat, but on carefully lifting it I can see the dough has puffed up a little. Not enough yet; the cupboard must be a little cooler today.

To distract myself I make a mug of coffee, and try to relax.

The clock slows down – why does it always do that?

Fifteen minutes pass sluggishly, and then I recheck the contents of the bowl. "This is better," I say out loud. I carry the bowl into the kitchen. No need for sitting on the floor this time, as my dough only needs gentle pounding. (Can one pound something gently? Never mind, I know what I mean.)

I stretch and push the dough until it shrinks back into a ball, then bully it into the shapes I want. One block for the loaf tin, six smaller rounds for rolls. And, covered by the teacloth they go back into the cupboard and I go to sit and wait.

Now, as the yeast smell builds up again, I anticipate the final smell of hot bread and feel hungry. But I don't want to eat, in case I am too full to appreciate the warm, buttery bread spread with honey or eaten with cheese.

At least the waiting is shorter this time, and my beautifully risen bread goes into the hot oven.

I set a timer for twelve minutes, and then distract myself by preparing the tray – mug, teabag, plate, butter, cheese. Did it really only take me three minutes to do all that?

I put the butter back in the fridge to chill.

I check the clock, my watch, the timer. Still eight minutes to go. As my nose breathes in the scent, my stomach rumbles.

I wash the bowl, put away the scales and flour. I wipe down the kitchen tops again. I check the clock, my watch, the timer. I clear the draining board. My stomach talks to me again.

At last. I open the oven door carefully and take out one roll. I knock the bottom as I was shown years ago, and hear the satisfying hollow thud of baked bread. Out come the rolls. I remember to reset the timer for the loaf before cutting into a roll, adding the cold butter curls that quickly melt into the bread.

As I carry the tray to my seat I stop to take the first bite.

Ambrosia could not be as good as warm, fresh, buttery bread.

Exploring South Yorkshire

The bus travelled through green woodland, trees meeting overhead and birds soaring above. It wound up and down the hills, past incredible slopes filled with tiny houses hanging on to the ground and wonderful views of the river in the valley below.

The trees were waving in the soft breeze, and the glimpses of sunlight between the canopy made the leaves glow.

Then we left the woods behind, and began to meander through the twisty side-roads, surrounded by houses. The route went up, then down - at times I wished for a seat belt as I looked through the front window onto a steep lane, dropping away in front of us. Then suddenly, we arrived at the small town centre. A long flat road stretched along a valley.

I left the bus and began to explore the town. It was a fascinating mix of cheap shops and individual specialist shops. The greengrocers' had trays of local fruit ready to makes into jam, alongside exotic salad items. The local 'caff' was just down the road from the elegant coffee shop. There was an antique shop and a cheap range supermarket.

I stopped for a coffee and watched people pass by. They were like the town itself, a marvellous mix of different groups living together.

I would like to live here.

What, No 'Ats?

I recently moved to a small town in South Yorkshire. It is officially part of a 'deprived area', and the walk from my home into the town centre shows the signs of decay and a lack of investment.

But that is only part of the story. This Metropolitan District is mostly rural, and the older villages and the pit towns are surrounded by lush farmland and dense woods. There are stables with glossy horses, small holdings with chickens running free and fields full of green or pale gold crops.

And within the towns are classic churches and glimpses of tiny wynds with cottages. There are gardens resplendent with spring and then summer flowers.

And more important still, there are people who smile at strangers and say hello, or chat to me at bus stops and in shop queues.

Yes, there are the streets full of broken fences and graffiti; some areas I would not walk in at night. There are headlines about the evil; those living here with us who are the dangerous and depraved and their victims. But these are just part of the story.

Last summer I planned to travel along the bus routes, getting off every few stops to photograph the interesting, the beautiful and even the ugly; to show the mix of other things that make up the District I chose to live in; to show the wonderful mix of places that make up my adopted home.

I bought a real camera, the first one I'd ever owned.

I didn't finish it last year, in fact I barely made a start and since then one of the more scenic bus routes has disappeared - but this year I will go out so I can share my new home with others.

Ouch!

I was not a strong swimmer, but I enjoyed paddling around in the warm sea when we lived in the Caribbean.

I remember going out with my sister and a friend of my mother's to ride the waves. They dived under each wave, while I was lifted over. This was probably the furthest I had been from the shore, but tightly holding onto 'A' I felt safe.

Not always safe though. One day swimming in the shallow water with the other children I heard screaming. Looking round there was the lump of jelly; and I was the closest to it. I desperately tried to swim to shore, but it didn't feel as though I was moving away. The mass crept towards me, as time slowed. Then there was the agonising pain.

I don't remember how I got onto the beach, but there was mother pulling down my suit and rubbing harsh sand across my burning back. Once home, I was laid in bed on my stomach and washed with lime cologne. Then I spent two or three days in a darkened room.

It was the most painful thing I had ever endured; and I was never quite as comfortable in the sea afterwards.

But years later, hearing people in England spread rumours and fear about killer jellyfish seen nearby, I could say 'I was stung by a Portuguese Man o' War once'.

Note - *Just in case you are ever stung. Do not rub yourself with sand, and do not rub in cologne afterwards! Our knowledge increases and advice changes – and now we know that both of these actions ensure the pain will be worse and last longer!*

Work, 1970s Style

I joined the Civil Service in 1970, fresh from school. It was my first proper, grown-up job but it wasn't always obvious I'd left school as we had lots of school-like rules.

In those days girls wore dresses to school, no trousers. And in the Civil Service women were not permitted to wear trousers; we could wear 'ladies' suits with skirts, or dresses, but no trousers.

We had a canteen, much like the school canteen although there was a small bar next to it. And the food was a little better.

We called our bosses 'sir', and they sat in splendid isolation in large offices on another floor, each protected by a secretary in the outer office.

We had strict times to arrive and leave; intended, so they said, to stagger exits from the car park. My start time was 08.28. I never found out why mine was 8.28 and not 8.27 or 8.29.

We got annual reports. (This was not common then.)

We endured the sexism. And the rest - I was advised never to get in a lift with one of the bosses after lunch, but no one spoke to him or tried to stop it. You are shocked this felt like school? Where my English teacher used to stand behind us as we bent over our desks, looking down the front of our uniform dresses to see our bras. He'd done it for years.

But it wasn't all the same.

I sat with the Geeks on the fourth floor; a geek-only floor where some men wore cravats instead of ties. Where some women wore mini skirts; not quite flouting the dress code but only because it hadn't caught up with fashion.

If remarks were made, we'd smile apologetically and explain it was this or trousers, we didn't own anything else.

A small freedom.

The Mighty Heap

For a few months I worked as a gardener.

I do not have green thumbs, I have black, plant-murdering thumbs, but my children kept growing and we needed some extra money. And most importantly, any work had to fit around my mother's part-time job so I could get free childcare.

I somehow passed the interview and started work. On the first day he showed me the petrol mower; I'd never seen one close up before. Each week I would approach it cautiously and gently pull the string to start it, and then pull it harder, and then harder. Then I mowed his lawn.

Up to two hours of cutting grass.

I would empty the bin into a wheelbarrow, and when the barrow was full I would push it up to the compost heap. A magnificent heap at least 12 feet high and probably about 18 feet in diameter. My living room would have been lost under it. I'd push the barrow up to the top, tip the cuttings out then back to the lawn and more grass, back up the slope of the heap, to the top, and more green cuttings heaved over.

In the autumn I would sweep up leaves, sometimes for my full two hours. Barrow loads of leaves pushed up to the top of the heap and tipped over the other side.

We never used any of the compost, yet my efforts barely increased its size.

The heap was the largest one in the town. It may have been the largest in the UK. In the world. All that rich leaf mould and grass just building up over the years. Smelling of rich loam, just waiting to be spread over the soil.

Taunting his small sparse flower beds that we both neglected.

I wonder if it is still there.

Acquiring Your First Cat

The parents of a friend 'let' their cat have kittens.
A few weeks go by, and then they suggest that their child invites a friend home for tea.

You arrive, to be fed cake and then allowed to cuddle one of the kittens. An hour or so goes by and it is time to go home, but now you don't want to put the kitten down.

"That is OK, why don't you take this one home?"
"Well, my mother might not agree."
"No problem, you can just take it home for tonight, and if your mother doesn't agree you can bring it back later."

Next thing you know they have found a suitable box, from a pile near the front door, and you are carrying the box home with a kitten mewling inside it and a tin of cat food in your school bag.

Your mother takes one look inside and says "No!" But there is the kitten curled up in the house for the night, and all the next day.

By the time you 'could' have returned it, it is too late.

About five months later your little kitten, now a cat, gives birth to some furry little kittens.

And six weeks later your mother suggests, quite firmly, that you invite some friends round, one at a time.

You notice your mother has started to collect small cardboard boxes.

Shared Gremlins?

I was watching TV this morning when the picture and sound disappeared to be replaced by a message that there was no signal. After a minute or so the programme restarted.

Strange I thought, and then forgot it.

Then Dad phoned me, from America, and told me all about setting up his new TV – delivered yesterday and full of extra IT.

A couple of hours later my son arrived for a brief visit, and, while here, he moved my TV – just a couple of centimetres so he could watch it. And the signal went off again.

But this time it didn't come back. When he checked behind it the aerial lead was out. He pushed it back in, but still nothing.

I did a retune – still nothing. We checked wires, and then turned it off and on (after all TVs are really computers nowadays). Nothing.

We gave up, and I started looking for free online TV streaming. As soon as I found a site I liked and started watching the news the TV restarted itself.

Two hours later Dad phoned to tell me that his new TV had stopped working a couple of hours earlier.

And Finally a Few Filks

Not all Filks are TTTO*, to the tune of, but these are

Inspired by Another's Filk
Wights

Wights in night satin
for it's Halloween.
Children out begging,
full of cookies and cream.

Babies I've always loved,
so tender and warm.
Sharpen your teeth dears,
get ready to swarm.

For we want you
yes we want you
oh how we want you

People in doorways,
like cattle in pens.
Come now my sisters,
crawl out of your dens.

Children wrapped warmly,
so juicy and fresh.
Dinner is served up,
such succulent flesh.

For we want you
yes we want you
oh how we want you
Big Hunter

The second you jumped from that ship
I could tell you were a famous traveller
a real big hunter
great muscles, so sublime
now wouldn't you need to know what's going on over here

Well let me get into your mind
I can see whatever you want me to see
so big hunter
buy a little time from me

Wouldn't you like a few beads, big beads
how about a new hat, hat, hats?
I can sell you some nice masks
And I'll give you a good price

The second you jumped from that ship
I could tell you were a famous traveller
a real big hunter
great muscles so sublime
now wouldn't you need to know what's going on over here

Well let me get into your mind
I can see whatever you want me to see
so big hunter
now big hunter
yes big hunter

buy a little time from me

Dreams

You filled up my bathtub
with soft frothy bubbles
you brought me a warm towel
scented with rose
you made me fresh coffee
with dark chocolate sprinkles
you played me our music
a long loud deep purr

Oh how I love you
my dark-haired young feline
your soft furry body
your generous gifts
oh how I love you
my bright little kitten
as you purr in my ears
at twenty to five.

You filled up my bathtub
with soft frothy bubbles
you brought me a warm towel
scented with rose
you made me fresh coffee
with dark chocolate sprinkles
you played me our music
a long loud deep purr

and woke me up

Printed in Great Britain
by Amazon